Five Little Monkeys Jumping on the Bed

Retold and Illustrated by
EILEEN CHRISTELOW

Clarion Books
New York

For

Heather   Morgan

Joni

Grady   Stefan

———————————————

Clarion Books
an imprint of Houghton Mifflin Harcourt Publishing Company
215 Park Avenue South, New York, NY 10003
Copyright © 1989 by Eileen Christelow

www.clarionbooks.com

Printed in Malaysia.

Library of Congress Cataloging-in-Publicaton Data
Christelow, Eileen.
Five little monkeys jumping on the bed / retold and illustrated by Eileen Christelow.
p. cm.
Summary: A counting book in which one by one the little monkeys jump on the bed
only to fall off and bump their heads.
ISBN 0-89919-769-8
[1. Monkeys—Fiction. 2. Counting] I. Title. II. Title: 5 little monkeys jumping on the bed.
PZ7.C4523Fi   1989
[E]—dc19
88-22839
CIP   AC

CL ISBN-13: 978-0-89919-769-2
PA ISBN-13: 978-0-395-55701-3

TWP   55 54 53 52
4500214768

It was bedtime. So five little monkeys took a bath.

Five little monkeys put on their pajamas.

Five little monkeys brushed their teeth.

Five little monkeys said good night to their mama.

Then...five little monkeys jumped on the bed!

One fell off and bumped his head.

The mama called the doctor. The doctor said,

"No more monkeys jumping on the bed!"

12

So four little monkeys...

...jumped on the bed.

One fell off and bumped his head.

The mama called the doctor.   The doctor said,

"No more monkeys jumping on the bed!"

So three little monkeys jumped on the bed.

One fell off and bumped her head.

The mama called the doctor.

The doctor said,

20

"No more monkeys jumping on the bed!"

So two little monkeys jumped on the bed.

One fell off and bumped his head.

The mama called the doctor.

The doctor said,

"No more monkeys jumping on the bed!"

So one little monkey jumped on the bed.

She fell off and bumped her head.

The mama called the doctor.

The doctor said,

"NO MORE MONKEYS JUMPING ON THE BED!"

So five little monkeys fell fast asleep.

"Thank goodness!" said the mama.

"Now I can go to bed!"